A Gift for:
♥ Lil Ziggy ♥
Date: 4 · 4 · 2022
With Love, Auntie Ashlee ♥
D1608743

This Book is Inspired by and Dedicated to:

My Niece, Julia Marie Lee.
I am so incedibly proud of you in every tense; past, present and future.
I cherish watching you weave your dreams into reality. (I love you more and it's in print!)

To my Niece, Monet Victoria Lee, and my Nephew, Grayson Michael Lee.
May your minds always wonder and your hearts always sing.

To my Mom, you are my guiding light, my touchstone, compass and role model.
Thank you for always believing in me, without your love and unwavering confidence I'd be lost.

To my Best Friend and Husband, Buck, I love you and I'm so lucky to share this life with you.
Thank you for putting up with me and being the best human in general.

To my Brother and Sister-In-Law, Warren and Sheila, you are both the best and
thank you so much for the greatest gift of making me an Aunt tree times!

To Mom # 2, Cheryl, thank you so much for your unwavering love and support.
You are one of the greatest treasures in our lives.

To my Aunt Kathie, growing up you were my inspiration and taught me how to have fun.
I am so thankful for having you in my life and for the impacts you've made,
you truly helped to shape me into the woman I am today.

To all my friends out there, thank you so much for all the love and always supporting me!
(You know who you are.)

To my neighbor, Laurel. You know why.

To my Father-In-Law, Mike Prichard,
we miss you every day and I love you more than words can express.

Art and Words by J. L. Prichard

ISBN 978-0-578-28144-5 (paperback)

Published by J. L. Prichard Press

Written and Illustrated
by J.L. Prichard

Hi!

This is Julia.

Anyone can live in

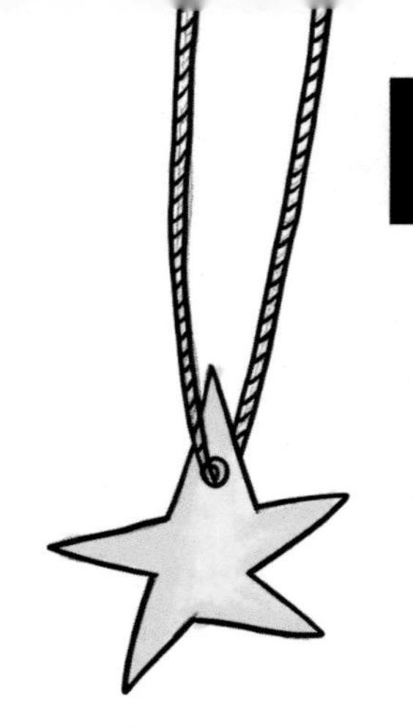

The Outside World is Black and White.
Anything is Possible in Julia's Wold.

Apples are as **BIG** as houses

and the Moon is made of **Cheese**

and covered by Mouses.

The Correct Word is Mice

when there is more than one mouse.

The Mice eat the Cheese on the Moon Every Night

and it becomes Smaller

and Smaller with Every Last Bite.

In Julia's World
An Apple is as BIG
as a House you see,

To a Worm
it's a Place
for his Family
to be.

In Julia's World

The Grass is many colors except Green

and My-Oh-My it's a Sight to be Seen!

It's Yellows, Purples, Oranges and Blues

and when you walk it leaves the colors

on the Bottoms of your Shoes!

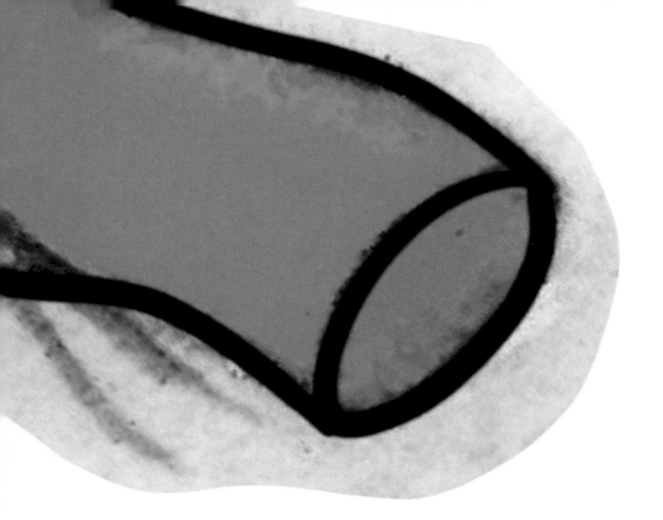

In Julia's World

Unicorns play with Poodles.

They love to float around all day

in the Pool with their Noodles!

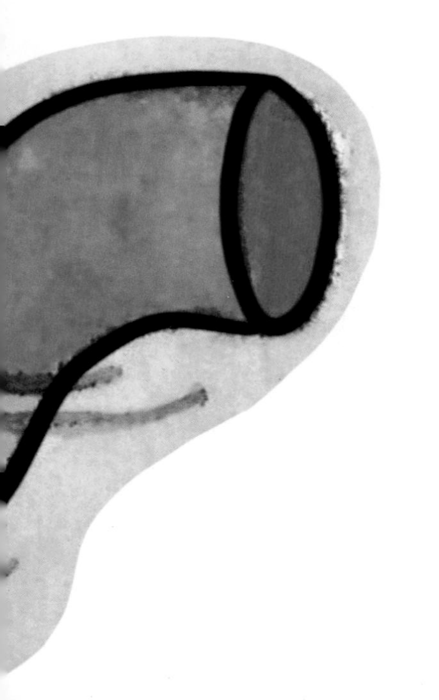

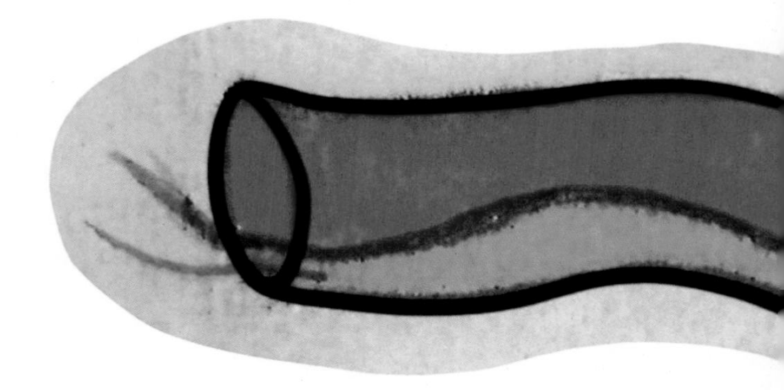

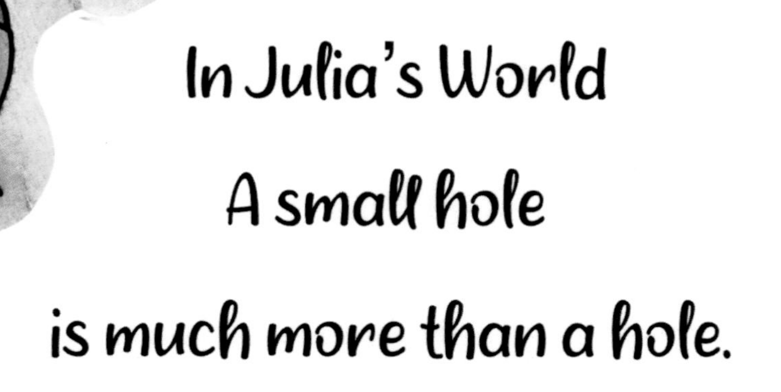

In Julia's World

A small hole

is much more than a hole.

Julia knows,

that if you looked in

you'd be Surprised

to learn of the Life of a Mole.

In Julia's World

She takes a Ride on a Dragonfly.

As they Dance in the Wind

They watch the Whole World pass them by.

In Julia's World
Her Dog
named "Oreo"
talks.

They have

In-Depth

Coversations

about Life

on their Walks.

In Julia's World

When she looks into the Clouds

and sees a Fox

It comes to Life

and she names him Socks!

In Julia's World

The Trees Sing in the Breeze.

They Sway Back and Forth

to their Sweet Melodies!

In Julia's World

Everyone is Friends

from First Glance.

No matter

how strange

the Circumstance.

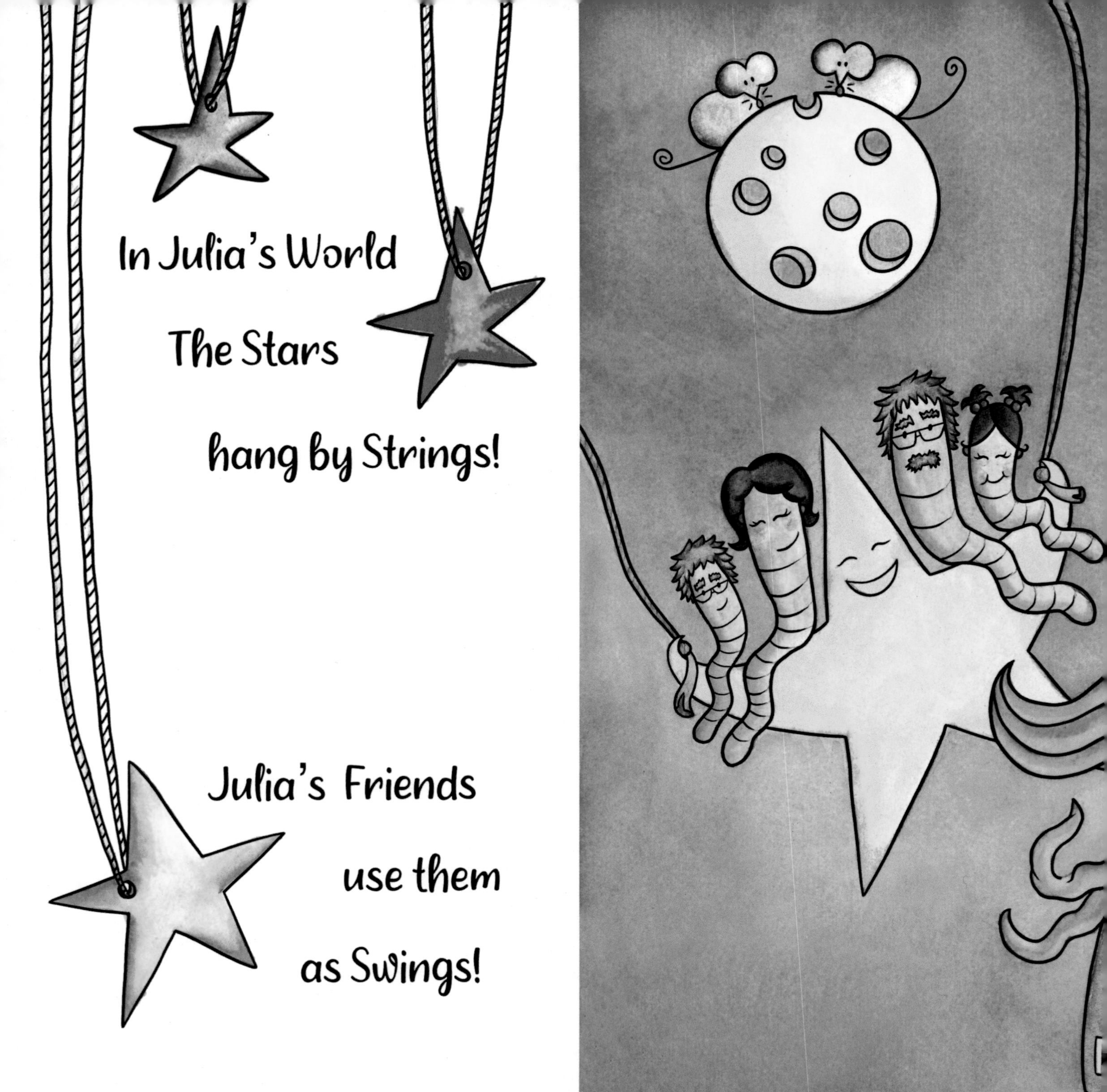

In Julia's World

The Stars

hang by Strings!

Julia's Friends

use them

as Swings!

Anyone can Live in a World of their Own,

Imagination

is the Key.

So just close your eyes and Imagine

How you want YOUR World to be.

__________________'s

World

Draw you!

Who lives in YOUR World?

Draw YOUR World!

What do you do for fun in your World?

Made in the USA
Columbia, SC
30 March 2022